Carter, Anne Laurel.

Under a prairie sky.

$16.95

3254716014120

DATE			

Under a Prairie Sky

Under a Prairie Sky

Story by Anne Laurel Carter

Illustrations by Alan and Lea Daniel

ORCA BOOK PUBLISHERS

For Ann Featherstone, and my little brother Jim
A. L. C.

For Carolynn and Steve
A. & L. Daniel

National Library of Canada Cataloguing in Publication

Carter, Anne, 1953-
Under a prairie sky / story by Anne Laurel Carter;
illustrations by Alan and Lea Daniel.
Reading grade level: 3-4.
For ages 6-10.
ISBN 1-55143-226-9 (bound) ISBN 1-55143-282-X (pbk.)

1. Prairie Provinces—Juvenile fiction. 2 Royal Canadian Mounted Police—Juvenile fiction. 3. Rescues—Juvenile fiction. 4. Picture books for children. I. Daniel, Alan, 1939- II. Daniel, Lea III. Title.

PS8555.A7727U52 2001 jC813'.54 C2001-910591-6

First published in the United States, 2002

Library of Congress Catalog Card Number: 2001097694

Orca Book Publishers gratefully acknowledges the support of our publishing programs provided by the following agencies: the Department of Canadian Heritage, The Canada Council for the Arts, and the British Columbia Arts Council.

Design by Alan Daniel
Printed and bound in Hong Kong

Orca Book Publishers
PO Box 5626, Station B
Victoria, BC Canada
V8R 6S4

Orca Book Publishers
PO Box 468
Custer, WA USA
98240-0468

06 05 04 03 • 5 4 3 2 1

When I grow up,
I'm going to be
a Mountie.

But today
I have to help Dad
harvest the wheat.

We work all day.
My black horse, Bess,
watches and waits.

Where's Will?" Dad asks.
My little brother
has disappeared.

Dad looks at the late-
afternoon sky.
"Storm's coming.
Better find your brother."

I run to the stable,
put on
my red serge coat
and Stetson hat,
blue breeches
and polished boots.
I saddle up Bess.

We march on
the prairie, ready.

This is a job for a
Mountie.

I search among
the yellow stooks
of drying wheat
where little brothers
like to hide.
"Where are you, Will?"

Tall elevators
beside the train tracks,
I thread my way
between them, looking,
looking for Will.
He's hard to find,
a needle in a grainstack.
But I'm on his trail.

"You can't hide
from a Mountie," I call.
I know he hears me.

My brother Will
roams free, like the ghost
of Old Buck,
the legendary bronco
who carried the bugle boy
on the Great March West
when the Mounties
brought law and order
to the frontier.

I'm on Will's trail.
I'll get my man.

I ride down the coulee,
to the valley
where Saskatoon berries
grow purple and sweet.
He's left a bucketful,
an easy clue.

A coyote calls.
I take up my lance and cry,
"Never fear. I'll protect you."

Charge!

Who's that?
Hiding beyond the dome
of willow branches?

"Out of there, you villain!
I've got you cornered."
But it's only a heron,
creeping away on stilts.

Will's trail grows cold,
but I won't give up.
"Come on, Bess.
Duty calls."
My boots are high,
my pennons white and red.

We canter across the wide
open spaces.
This is the land
where giants ride
and little brothers hide
in wagonwheels,
looking for buffalo heads.

I find him catching frogs
in the slough.
He tries to squirm away
with a grin.

"I've got you now," I say.
"Storm's coming, Will.
We've got to get home."

Bess runs, fast and sleek.

Dark clouds chase.

Thundering outlaws shoot
across the sky.

Pow!

Bolts of lightning fire
at us, hail on our heels.

Ping!

Mom and Dad are waiting.
We ride past, into the barn.

"Safe," Will says, reaching up.
"Close call."

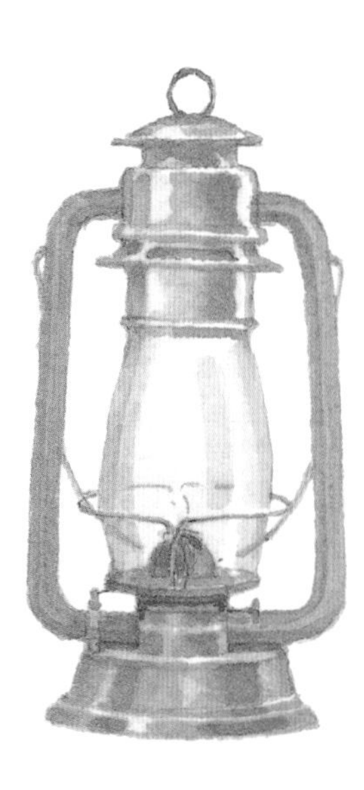

He steals my hat
with that grin!
Runs to the house,
protected
by my Stetson's brim,

leaving me
to brush down Bess.
My black beauty
stamps her foot at him,
but I just laugh.

"All in the line of duty,
Bess."

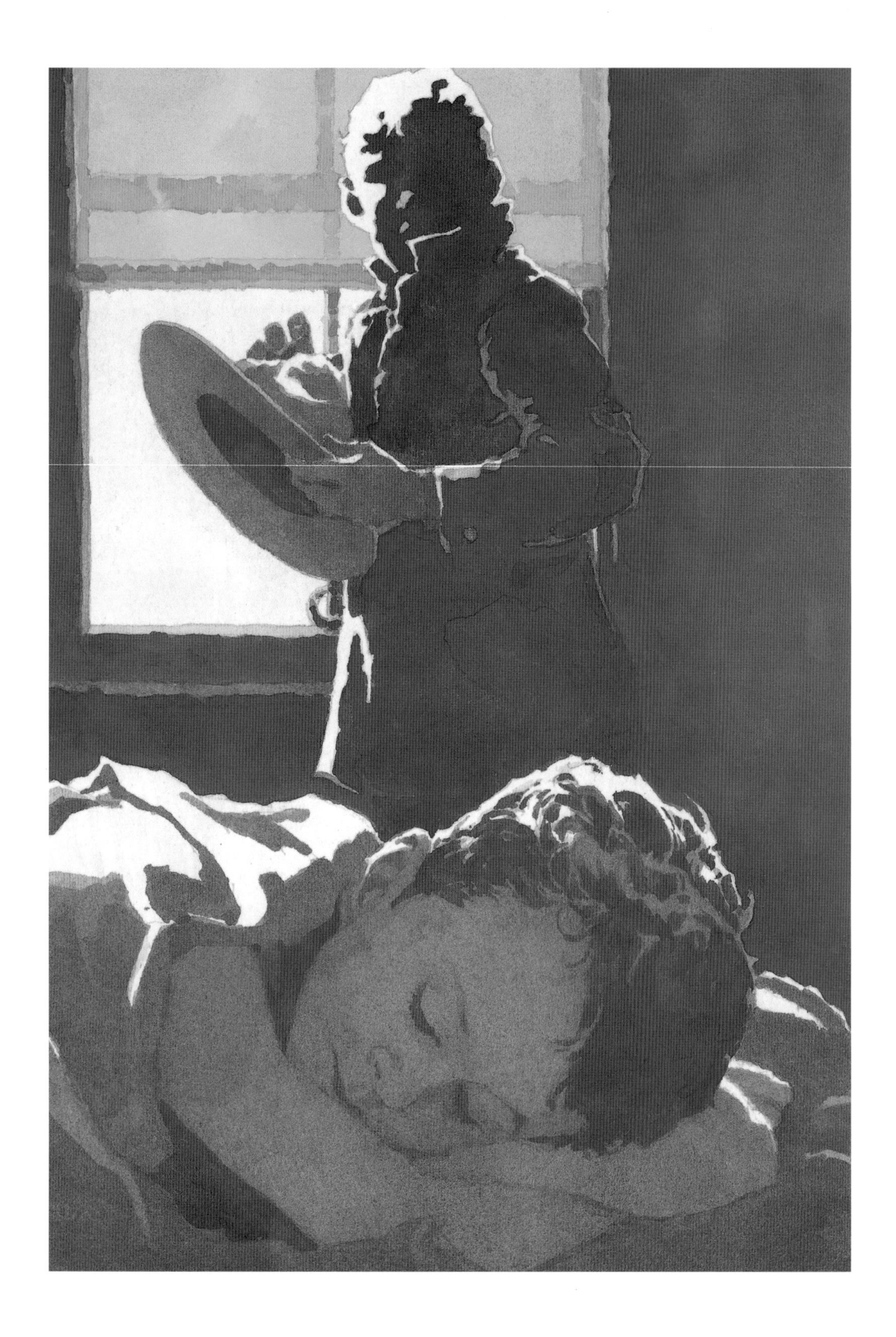

One day,
I'll be a Mountie,
patrol the land
where giants -
and little brothers -
sleep
under a prairie sky.